For Mum and Dad

First published 2014 by Walker Books Ltd

87 Vauxhall Walk, London SE11 5HJ

2 4 6 8 10 9 7 5 3 1

Text and illustrations © 2014 Alex Milway

The right of Alex Milway to be identified as the author and illustrator
of this work has been asserted by him in accordance with the
Copyright, Designs and Patents Act 1988

This book has been typeset in Burbank Big Regular

Printed and bound in China by South China Printing

British Library Cataloguing in Publication Data:
a catalogue record for this book is available from the British Library

ISBN 978-1-4063-4603-9

www.walker.co.uk

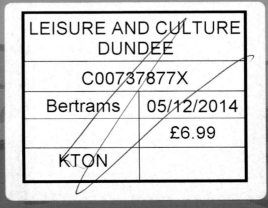

PIGSTICKS AND HAROLD

AND THE TUPTOWN THIEF

Alex Milway

WALKER
BOOKS

A case for Pigsticks

It was the day before the Butterfly Ball, and Pigsticks and Harold couldn't wait. There would be cake, games, amazing butterflies — and best of all, someone would win the Spirit of Tuptown Prize for being brilliant.

Milton Rhino, the mayor of Tuptown, called a meeting at his house to plan the big day. He gave everyone a job to do.

Milton asked Harold to make a statue for the winner of the Spirit of Tuptown Prize. Harold was very excited.

Harold worked all through the night to finish the statue in time. Apart from his famous Battenburg cake, it was the best thing he'd ever made.

8

At last, the statue was ready. Harold wrapped it

up so it would be a surprise on the big day.

The next morning, when Harold went outside to check on the statue, he made a shocking discovery. It had disappeared! "Where's it gone?" thought Harold. "I definitely left it here."

Harold rushed to Pigsticks' house – he always knew what to do.

Pigsticks and Milton were practising their speeches for the Ball when Harold arrived.

"The Spirit of Tuptown statue is gone!" cried Harold. "This is all that's left – a measly ribbon!"

"Wait a minute..." said Pigsticks. "It looks like that ribbon has been cut with scissors."

"You're not saying—" said Milton.

"I am," said Pigsticks. "The statue has been stolen!"

"NO!" cried Harold. He was horrified. There had never been a thief in Tuptown before.

"We need a first-class detective," said Pigsticks.

"Do you know one?" said Milton.

"Know one?" said Pigsticks. "I am one."

"Have you ever actually solved a crime?" asked Harold.

"I solved **THE GREAT TRAIN ROBBERY** ...

and **THE CASE OF THE MISSING BIRTHDAY CAKE** ...

and **THE MYSTERY OF THE SNORING HEDGE!**"

Harold hadn't realized his friend was so talented.

Pigsticks really was a first-class detective.

PIG DADDY

ERNEST HEMINGPIG

HERCULE PIGOT

Great Uncle
Hercule Pigot would
be very proud!

"We will track down the thief and find the statue!" said Pigsticks.

"We?" said Harold.

"Yes! Every good detective needs an assistant," said Pigsticks. "I am the best detective, so I need the best assistant!"

"Who is that?" asked Harold.

"You, of course," said Pigsticks.

"You will make a great team," said Milton.

"We always do," said Pigsticks.

"I'm not sure about this," said Harold. "I can barely catch a cold, let alone a thief."

"But we can't let the thief get away with it!" said Pigsticks. "Without the statue, there will be no Spirit of Tuptown Prize. And without the Spirit of Tuptown Prize, the Ball will be ruined. We must be brave! You are no mere hamster. You are Harold."

Harold realized

Pigsticks was right.

I AM HAROLD!

"Now we just need to look the part," said Pigsticks.

He disappeared into his wardrobe and returned

with detective clothes.

DEERSTALKER HAT
Official headgear of the serious detective

MAGNIFYING GLASS
Helps you see evidence clearly

NOTEBOOK
To write all of Pigsticks' observations in

"Don't I get a cape?" asked Harold.

"Only proper detectives get one of those," said Pigsticks.

Milton slapped Pigsticks and Harold on the back. "Good luck, team," he said.

"We don't need luck," said Pigsticks. "We are the best detectives the world has ever seen! Come on, Harold. We have a crime to solve!"

The plot thickens

Pigsticks and Harold headed straight for Harold's garden: the scene of the crime.

"Every thief leaves clues," said Pigsticks. "You take notes. I'll be doing more important things."

Harold wrote that down so he wouldn't forget.

"This is a very difficult case," said Pigsticks.

"We'll need to interview everyone in Tuptown.

Anyone could be the thief!"

"Even you or me?" said Harold.

"We can't rule ourselves out," said Pigsticks.

By the time they reached the town centre, everybody had heard about the stolen statue.

"No one can leave town tonight," said Pigsticks.

"The thief is among us ..."

Pigsticks started interviewing suspects right away.

SISSY PORCUPINE

Envious of my artistic skills

BONZO

Has access to cutting tools

PIRATE GEORGE

Why is he always so happy?

BENJAMIN HORSE

What does he keep under that blazer?

Everyone seemed to have a motive.

"How will we ever find the thief?" wondered

Harold. There was something suspicious about

everybody in Tuptown.

EVIE BIRD

Stronger than
she looks

OTTERLY

Is the
tail mark in
my garden
hers?

**ALICE
ANTEATER**

Could have
cut ribbon
with claws

BOBBINS
(THE ANGRY MOUSE)

Hates
everything

**MILTON
RHINO**

Collects statues
(lots of them)

Just then, Sissy came running towards them.

"All of my fruit has vanished!" she cried. "Even the gooseberries! They've been stolen!"

"The plot thickens," said Pigsticks.

"It's probably for the best," said Harold.

"Gooseberries do spoil a good pudding."

Someone's pinched all my fruit!

"This is serious," said Sissy. "Without my fruit,
I can't make my famous Berry Surprise for the Ball!"

Harold hadn't thought of that.

"We have a new crime scene to investigate," said
Pigsticks. "Let's go to Sissy's garden! We'll need our
protective clothes so we don't spoil the evidence..."

Sissy's garden was full of clues.

"Look for anything that's out of place," said Pigsticks.

"Hmmmfff mmm hhm ffff," said Harold.

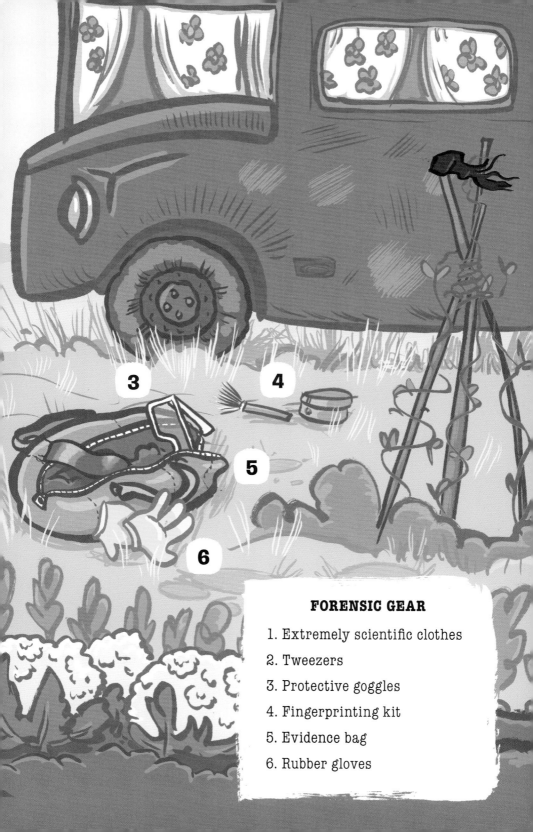

FORENSIC GEAR

1. Extremely scientific clothes
2. Tweezers
3. Protective goggles
4. Fingerprinting kit
5. Evidence bag
6. Rubber gloves

"Who are our main suspects?"
asked Pigsticks.

Harold looked at his notebook.

"Bonzo, Alice and Pirate George,"
said Harold. "They all wear red, and I
found red material in Sissy's garden."

But Pigsticks didn't agree. "It
must be Otterly or Bobbins," he said.

Pigsticks is probably right,
thought Harold. He is a proper
detective, after all.

DON'T FORGET TO MAKE NOTES,
PIGSTICKS SAYS SO!

THIEF WEARS RED!

CLAW FOOTPRINTS...

SQUISHED BERRIES -
  LOOK FOR STAINS!

WAS THAT FUR IN MY GARDEN?

fur   TAIL MARKS?

SHOPPING
LIST:
CAKE
BISCUITS
CREAM
STRAWBERRIES
SAWDUST

As Pigsticks and Harold were heading home,

Milton came charging down the road.

"They've gone!" said Milton.

"What's gone?" asked Harold.

"Look around!" said Milton. "What can't you see?"

"Lots of things," said Pigsticks. "For instance, I don't see any sandwiches."

"That's true," said Harold, suddenly hungry.

"No, no," said Milton. "What's missing?"

"The butterflies have disappeared!" said Harold. "What are we going to do? It's bad enough that the Spirit of Tuptown statue has gone, and there's no Berry Surprise to eat, but we definitely can't have a Butterfly Ball without butterflies!"

"This is the final straw," said Milton. "We will have to cancel everything!"

Harold was close to tears. All their detective work had been for nothing.

But Pigsticks wasn't giving up.

Hold it right there! This is not the end!

"We're Pigsticks and Harold," said Pigsticks. "We are never beaten! And we have one more trick up our sleeves!"

"What's that?" asked Harold.

"We'll go undercover! We'll wear amazing disguises and catch the thief red-handed," said Pigsticks.

"What disguises?" said Harold.

"You'll see," said Pigsticks. "I'll need a sewing machine and a lot of paint..."

I hate ice cream.

A twist in the tail

In no time at all, Pigsticks returned with the amazing disguises.

"No one will recognize us in these outfits!" he said. "I have designed them to lure the thief straight into our trap!"

"Here's the plan," said Pigsticks. "You two will blend into the background and look out for the thief. And I will be the bait in the trap!"

"The bait?" said Harold. "That sounds dangerous!"

"Danger's my middle name," said Pigsticks.

"I thought it was Endeavour?" said Harold.

"I have many middle names," said Pigsticks.

"Now, let's go outside. You two stand still, and I will

flutter like a butterfly. With any luck, the thief will

try to steal me."

Pigsticks and his undercover agents waited and waited. The sun went down, and a bright moon took its place. Harold stood as still as he could ... and soon he got the feeling that someone was watching them from the bushes.

"Pigsticks!" he whispered.

But his friend was fluttering too far away to hear.

"Milton! Pigsticks is in danger!" he hissed.

"I can't move in this stupid tree suit!" said Milton.

"It's down to you!"

Harold had to warn Pigsticks – fast.

But he was too late. Pigsticks was gone, and Harold was alone in the dark. "I knew I wouldn't make a good detective's assistant," he thought.

Just then, he saw a shadowy figure in the darkness, coming closer and closer. It looked like a horrible monster. Harold stood terrified, frozen to the spot.

But it wasn't a monster — it was Pigsticks!

"You're alive!" said Harold. "How did you escape?"

"I scared the thief off with a terrifying squeal.

And now I know who it is!"

They raced to Milton's house. Milton was already there – and because Pigsticks had been kidnapped, he'd cancelled the Ball. Everyone was quite upset.

"Not so fast! I'm back!" said Pigsticks. "And I have solved the case!"

"You know who the thief is?" said Milton.

"Of course!" said Pigsticks.

"Pirate George!" cried Pigsticks. "Only you have the strength to kidnap a pig of my size!"

"No! He's innocent," said Otterly. "He's been with me all night, singing sea shanties!"

"Oh," said Pigsticks. "Are you sure? Er..."

Just then, Harold pulled Pigsticks aside and gave him his notebook. "This might help," he whispered.

Pigsticks closed the notebook. "As I was saying," he said, "it all started when the statue was stolen. We thought the ribbon was cut with scissors. In fact, the thief had sharp claws. Then, when we interviewed everyone, we noticed orange peel in our suspect's pocket – just before Sissy announced her fruit had been stolen. And then, when we went undercover, we spotted a butterfly in the thief's house."

"So who is it?" asked Milton.

"Let's go to the town hall," said Pigsticks. "All will be revealed..."

1. SHARP CLAWS

2. ORANGE PEEL IN POCKET

3. BUTTERFLY IN HOUSE

"The thief has one last thing planned," whispered Pigsticks.

He opened the door as quietly as he could. Everyone held their breath...

"Alice! You're the thief?" gasped Milton.

Alice nodded. "I never meant to cause so much trouble," she said. "It all began when everyone got a job to do for the Ball – apart from me. I felt left out. I wanted to prove I could do something all by myself, so I organized the whole party.

"Once I stole the statue, I just couldn't stop myself ... it was a slippery slope from there.

"I didn't mean to kidnap Pigsticks. I thought he was a very heavy butterfly. I'm so sorry. What can I do to make up for everything I've done?"

Milton cleared his throat. "Actually, Alice, I hadn't forgotten you. I've got a very important job for you — and I've been saving it till last."

"Really?" said Alice.

"Of course!" said Milton. "I'd like you to choose the winner of the Spirit of Tuptown Prize!"

Alice was overjoyed. "You'd really let me do that?" she said.

"Absolutely," said Milton. "As long as you promise never to steal anything ever again. So, who are you going to choose?"

"Ladies and Gentlepigs," said Alice. "I am proud to say that the winner of this year's Spirit of Tuptown Prize is ... Pigsticks! For being a brilliant detective!"

Pigsticks smiled modestly. "I am the obvious choice!" he said. "But behind every pig is a trusty hamster. I am going to share this award with Harold - Tuptown's most brilliant detective's assistant."

Harold blushed, too happy to speak. He'd never won anything before.

"Now," said Pigsticks, "Harold and I would like to say a few words. I would like to thank Alice for giving us this prize. And Harold would like to thank me, for ... everything, really. So thank you – and thank me."

Everyone gave them a standing ovation.

"You did your job perfectly, Alice," said Milton. "Now everyone get ready. It's time to ..."

Everyone in Tuptown danced and sang and ate Berry Surprise all night long.

Just before it was time to go home, Pigsticks picked up the microphone.

"People of Tuptown: against all the odds, this has been the best Butterfly Ball in history. And to celebrate, I'd like to sing you all a little song I've written. My friends, this song is for you."